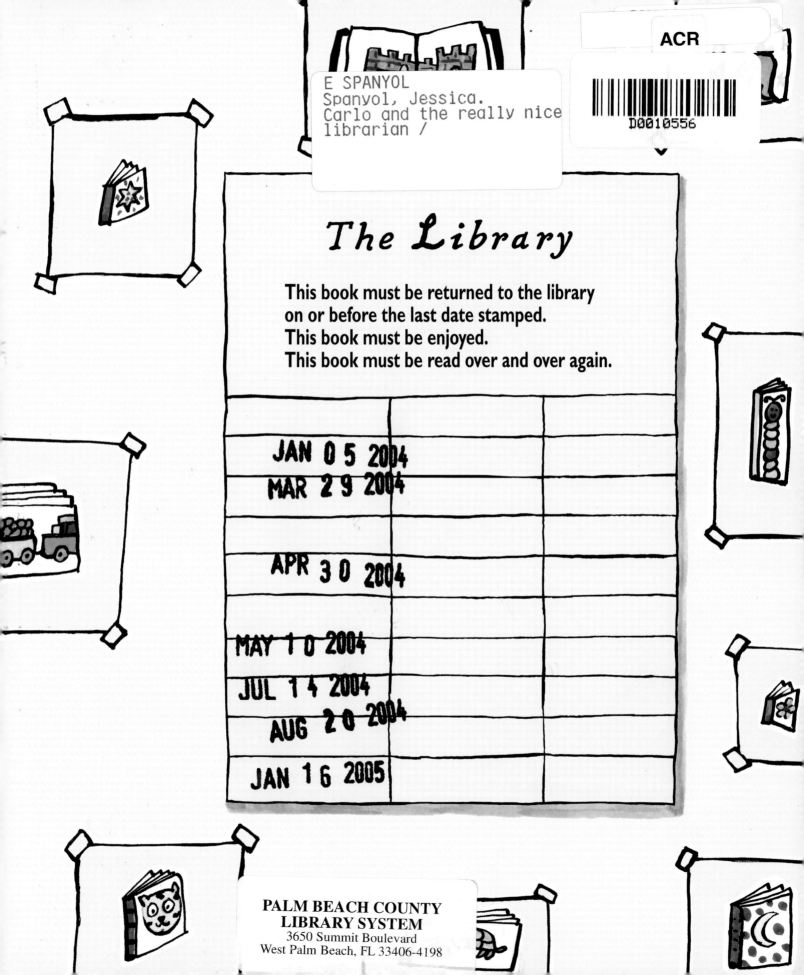

E SPANYOL
Spanyol, Jessica.
Carlo and the really nice
librarian /

ACR

D0010556

The Library

This book must be returned to the library
on or before the last date stamped.
This book must be enjoyed.
This book must be read over and over again.

JAN 0 5 2004		
MAR 2 9 2004		
APR 3 0 2004		
MAY 1 0 2004		
JUL 1 4 2004		
AUG 2 0 2004		
JAN 1 6 2005		

**PALM BEACH COUNTY
LIBRARY SYSTEM**
3650 Summit Boulevard
West Palm Beach, FL 33406-4198

Copyright © 2004 by Jessica Spanyol

All rights reserved. No part of this book may be reproduced, transmitted,
or stored in an information retrieval system in any form or by any means, graphic,
electronic, or mechanical, including photocopying, taping, and recording,
without prior written permission from the publisher.

First U.S. edition 2004

Library of Congress Cataloging-in-Publication Data

Spanyol, Jessica.
Carlo and the really nice librarian / Jessica Spanyol. —1st U.S. ed.
p. cm.
Summary: When Carlo the giraffe and Crackers the cat visit the new library,
they meet Mrs. Chinca, a very friendly and helpful librarian.
ISBN 0-7636-2526-4
[1. Librarians—Fiction. 2. Libraries—Fiction. 3. Giraffe—Fiction. 4. Cats—Fiction.] I. Title.
PZ7.S7368Caj 2004
[E]—dc22   2003069623

2 4 6 8 10 9 7 5 3 1

Printed in China

This book was typeset in SpanyolBold.
The illustrations were done in watercolor, acrylic, ink, and collage.

Candlewick Press
2067 Massachusetts Avenue
Cambridge, Massachusetts 02140

visit us at www.candlewick.com

Carlo
and the Really Nice
Librarian

CANDLEWICK PRESS
CAMBRIDGE, MASSACHUSETTS

Jessica Spanyol

One day, Dad
took Carlo and
Crackers to
the new library.

"Wow!" said Carlo when he saw all the books.

Dad called after Carlo, "I'm going to be just around this corner if you need me."

The library was amazing.
There were colorful posters.
There were chairs
with wheels.

And there was the longest desk Carlo had ever seen. "Come on, Crackers," said Carlo.

"Wheee!"

Books In
· The Red Balloon
· Bugs
· My Kite
· Daisy

"Hello, I'm **Mrs. Chinca**.
What's your name?"
"Carlo," whispered Carlo.
"And who is this?"
asked **Mrs. Chinca**.

"That's Crackers. He's my cat."
Mrs. Chinca, the librarian,
seemed a little scary.

"What kinds of books do you like, Carlo?" asked **Mrs. Chinca.**

"All kinds," Carlo said quietly.

"Very good. Well, let me show you some of our library books. Come on, Carlo.

Follow me."

"This is a good bedtime story," said Mrs. Chinca.

"Just look at these beautiful pictures, Carlo."

"And this is a very exciting read."

Carlo couldn't believe how much *Mrs. Chinca* knew about books.

"This is one of my favorites,"
said **Mrs. Chinca** in a muffled voice.
"Oh, I have that one at home!"
Carlo said excitedly.

Carlo was beginning to think that
Mrs. Chinca wasn't so scary after
all. She was being such a good
and helpful librarian.

"Would you like to read
a book with me?"
Mrs. Chinca asked Carlo.
Carlo thought that
would be fun.

"*Brmm brmm,*" he said
when he saw the cars.
"*Tick tock,*" he said when he
saw the clock.

"ROAR!"

said **Mrs. Chinca** when she saw the lion.

Carlo laughed so much he got his tail in a tangle!

Next, **Mrs. Chinca** asked Carlo to
help her. "You have such a lovely
long neck, Carlo. Could you put
these books on the top shelf?"
Carlo really liked helping **Mrs. Chinca**.

Then **Mrs. Chinca** gave Carlo
his very own library card.

"Thank you so much!"
exclaimed Carlo.

index cards

keys

Mrs. Chinca's
purse

APPLICATION
The Library
NAME: Carlo
ADDRESS: 4 Valentine Road

pencil
sharpener

library card

Mrs. Chinca's pens
and pencils

rubber stamp

After Carlo had finished choosing his books,
Dad said it was time to go home.
Carlo felt sad to leave.
He couldn't believe he had ever been
scared of *Mrs. Chinca.*

Mrs. Chinca used Carlo's new library card
to check out all his books.
"Bye-bye, Carlo. Bye-bye, Crackers.
See you again soon," she said.
"Bye-bye, Mrs. Chinca," said Carlo.

Books Out
· The Garden
· Baby Owls
· Tweet Tweet
· Hello, Robots
· Isabella Pig
· Shapes
· Trevor the Spider

As soon as Carlo got home, he told Mom all about *Mrs. Chinca*. "She's really nice and a lot of fun," said Carlo. "She sounds wonderful," said Mom.

Then Carlo showed Mom his library books. It wasn't until Carlo opened his last book that he noticed something strange. . . .

There was a tiny
bite-size piece missing!

"Mrs. Chinca really does love her books,"
said Carlo with a laugh.